ENCYCLOPEDIA BROWN

Solves Them All

By Donald J. Sobol

The Double Quest
The Lost Dispatch
The First Book of Medieval Man
Two Flags Flying
A Civil War Sampler
The Wright Brothers at Kitty Hawk
The First Book of the Barbarian Invaders
Stocks and Bonds (with Rose Sobol)
An American Revolutionary War Reader
Lock, Stock, and Barrel
The Strongest Man in the World
Two-Minute Mysteries
Secret Agents Four
Greta the Strong
Milton the Model A
More Two-Minute Mysteries
Encyclopedia Brown, Boy Detective
Encyclopedia Brown and the Case of the Secret Pitch
Encyclopedia Brown Finds the Clues
Encyclopedia Brown Gets His Man
Encyclopedia Brown Keeps the Peace
Encyclopedia Brown Lends a Hand
Encyclopedia Brown Saves the Day
Encyclopedia Brown Shows the Way
Encyclopedia Brown Solves Them All
Encyclopedia Brown Takes the Case
Encyclopedia Brown Tracks Them Down

Weekly Reader Books presents

Ten all-new Mysteries
ENCYCLOPEDIA BROWN
Solves Them All

by DONALD J. SOBOL

illustrated by Leonard Shortall

THOMAS NELSON INC.
Nashville / Camden / New York

For
My Son
Eric

This book is a presentation of
Weekly Reader Books.

Weekly Reader Books offers
book clubs for children from
preschool through junior high school.
All quality hardcover books are selected
by a distinguished Weekly Reader Selection Board.

For further information write to:
Weekly Reader Books
1250 Fairwood Ave.
Columbus, Ohio 43216

Library of Congress Catalog Card Number: 68–22746

ISBN 0–8407–7212–2

Printed in the United States of America

2 3 4 5 / 83 82 81 80

Contents

The Case of the Missing Clues

Although there are thousands of private detectives in the United States, the town of Idaville had but one.

Idaville did not need more. Its one detective was Encyclopedia Brown, and he had never lost a case.

Aside from Encyclopedia, Idaville was like most towns its size. It had three movie theaters, two delicatessens, and four banks. It had rich families and poor families. It had churches and synagogues, and a lovely beach which everyone could use.

And for more than a year, no grown-up or child had got away with breaking the law.

Encyclopedia's father was chief of the Idaville police. People across the country believed he was the best police chief in the world.

Chief Brown was proud of his record. He was proud of his men. But he was proudest of his only child, Encyclopedia.

Alas, Chief Brown had to keep his pride in Encyclopedia a secret. Whom could he tell? Who would believe him? Who would believe that the real mastermind behind Idaville's war on crime was ten years old!

Whenever the police came up against a puzzling case, Chief Brown knew where to go. He went home. Encyclopedia would solve the case during dinner in the Brown's red brick house on Rover Avenue.

Encyclopedia never whispered a word about the help he gave his father. He didn't want to seem different from other fifth graders.

But he was stuck with his nickname.

Only his parents and teachers called him by

his real name, Leroy. Everyone else in Idaville called him Encyclopedia.

An encyclopedia is a book or set of books filled with all kinds of facts. Encyclopedia had read more books than anyone in Idaville, and he never forgot what he read. He was the only library in America that could get around on a two-wheeler.

Between schoolwork and police work, Encyclopedia kept busy during the winter. During the summer he ran his own detective agency. He solved cases for the children of the neighborhood.

Every morning during the summer he hung his sign outside the garage:

BROWN DETECTIVE AGENCY
13 Rover Avenue
Leroy Brown, President
No case too small
25¢ per day
plus expenses

Early one afternoon a small boy pulled a red wagon into the Brown Detective Agency.

The wagon was loaded with fresh fruit. The boy was loaded with anger.

He slammed twenty-five cents onto the gasoline can beside Encyclopedia.

"My name is Abner Nelson," he said. "I want to hire you. I sell fruit."

"Is business dropping off?" said Encyclopedia.

"No, it's disappearing!" said Abner. "For the past two weeks a big kid comes to my stand every day. He helps himself to whatever he likes. And he doesn't pay!"

"You need protection," said Encyclopedia.

"Protection!" screamed Abner. "Oh, no! I want to be *protected* from protection!"

Abner explained. He grew the fruit in his back yard and sold it at a stand on Grant Road. Two weeks ago a big kid had stopped at the stand.

"He told me I needed protection," said Abner.

"From whom?" asked Encyclopedia.

"From other boys who have fruit stands during the summer," replied Abner. "The big kid said they might wreck my stand."

"So he offered to protect you?"

"Yes," said Abner. "He comes by every day with a big grin and brags about what a swell job he's doing of protecting me. 'Nobody has bothered you, right?' he says. Then he takes something to eat for his services."

"He's protecting you clean out of business," said Encyclopedia.

"I never needed him. He fooled me with his fast talk," said Abner. "You've got to stop him before he eats me into the poorhouse."

"What's his name?" said Encyclopedia.

"Bugs Meany."

"I might have guessed!" said Encyclopedia.

Bugs Meany was the leader of a gang of wild older boys. They called themselves the Tigers. They should have called themselves the Berries. They were always getting into one jam after another.

"That Bugs is awful tough," said Abner.

"Don't be afraid," said Encyclopedia. "I've dealt with him before. Let's hear what he has to say for himself."

"He won't say anything about the bag of cherries he took an hour ago," said Abner glumly.

The Tigers' clubhouse was an unused tool shed behind Mr. Sweeny's Auto Body Shop. When Encyclopedia and Abner arrived, Bugs was alone.

The Tiger leader was getting ready for school. He wasn't studying a book. He was studying a bicycle lock. He was teaching himself to open it with a hairpin.

Seeing Encyclopedia, he hastily shoved the hairpin into his pocket. "Make like a tree and leave," he snarled.

"First pay Abner here for all the fruit you've lifted from his stand," said Encyclopedia.

"You owe me three dollars and a quarter," said Abner. "And forty cents for the bag of cherries you took an hour ago. I never needed

THE CASE OF THE MISSING CLUES

your protection!"

"What's this? Protection? Bag of cherries?" cried Bugs. "Say, you two guys better not walk too close to a candy factory. They're looking for nuts like you."

Encyclopedia picked up a paper bag from the floor beside Bugs. Inside were three cherries.

"Where did you get these cherries?" demanded the boy detective.

Bugs worked hard at appearing calm. "Wh-why, I bought a pound of them at the super-market this morning."

"You mean you helped yourself to a pound from my fruit stand an hour ago!" said Abner.

"Listen," growled Bugs. "I've been right here in the clubhouse all afternoon, eating cherries and thinking. I don't know anything about protection, a fruit stand, or *your* bag of cherries."

"If that's true," said Encyclopedia, "you won't mind if I look around."

"Go right ahead," said Bugs. "Search till your eyeballs blister."

Encyclopedia ran his fingers over every inch of the floor.

The search did not take long. The clubhouse was tiny. The only bits of furniture were a carved up table and six orange crates which the Tigers used for chairs.

Encyclopedia got down on his hands and knees. He ran his fingers over every inch of the floor. He found seven nails, a clothes hanger, two comic books, three dried leaves, and a half inch of dirt and dust.

Next he turned to the wood box which the Tigers used as a wastebasket. It held two more comic books, an old newspaper, a rusty belt, and a broken checkerboard.

When Encyclopedia was finished with the wastebasket, he went outside.

Again he got down on all fours. He circled the clubhouse, digging his fingers into the grass and weeds. He touched every bit of ground for ten feet around the clubhouse.

Abner knelt beside him. "Are you looking for clues?"

Encyclopedia nodded, but did not reply.

"What did you find?" Abner pressed.

Encyclopedia opened his hand. "This," he said. On his palm were a piece of string, a paper clip, and several bubble-gum wrappers.

"There's nothing else around but plain old earth, grass, and weeds," said Encyclopedia.

Bugs sat down in the clubhouse doorway. He plucked a long stalk of grass and chewed on it triumphantly.

"Well, now, Mr. Brains," he said. "Did you find what you were looking for?"

"No," answered Encyclopedia. "And that proves you weren't in the clubhouse all afternoon!"

WHAT MISSING CLUES
PROVED BUGS LIED?

(*Turn to page 87 for the solution to the Case of the Missing Clues.*)

The Case of the Super-Secret Hold

The heart of Bugs Meany was filled with a great longing.

It was to knock Encyclopedia flatter than an elephant's instep.

Bugs hated being outsmarted by the boy detective. But whenever he felt like throwing a punch, he remembered Sally Kimball.

Sally was the prettiest girl in the fifth grade. It wasn't her face, however, that the toughest Tiger remembered. It was her fists.

Sally had done what no boy under fourteen had even dreamed of doing. She had outfought Bugs Meany.

Bugs told everyone that Sally had hit him with

a few lucky punches. Nobody believed his story, including Bugs himself. He thought she had hit him with a milk truck.

Because of Sally, Bugs never bullied Encyclopedia. Sally was the detective's junior partner.

"Bugs hates you more than he hates me," Encylopedia said as the partners sat in the Brown Detective Agency one afternoon. "You can be sure he'll try to get even."

Sally agreed. "He's like a thermometer in hottest Africa," she said. "He's always up to something."

Just then Duke Kelly, one of Bugs Meany's Tigers, entered the garage. He put twenty-five cents on the gasoline can. "Bugs wants you," he said.

"He wants to *hire us?*" gasped Sally.

"No, he wants you to come to the judo show this afternoon," said Duke. "The twenty-five cents will pay for your time."

Encyclopedia and Sally exchanged questioning glances.

"The judo show starts at two o'clock in the junior high school gym," said Duke.

"Judo?" Encyclopedia repeated half to himself. "The gentle art of self-defense?"

"Judo is the art of using your opponent's strength against him," said Duke, "or her."

With that he departed, grinning slyly.

"Bugs has more up his sleeve than his elbow," said Encyclopedia thoughtfully. "But I'm curious."

"So am I," said Sally. "Let's find out."

The junior high school gym was already filled with boys and girls when the detectives arrived. Coach Richards, who ran the summer sports program, spoke briefly. He explained the aims of judo.

Then four men from the Idaville Judo Center took places on the mat in the middle of the floor. They wore white trousers and a loose jacket bound at the waist by a knotted belt. For half an hour they demonstrated holds, locks, throws, and escapes.

After the children had stopped clapping, Coach Richards spoke again.

"Judo is not only for grown-ups," he said. "Three of our own junior high school students will now show you what they have learned in two short weeks."

Bugs Meany and two of his Tigers, Spike Larsen and Rocky Graham, trotted onto the mat. They wore the same white costumes as the men.

"Gosh, he's really good," said Sally as Bugs began flipping Spike and Rocky to the mat like baseball cards.

"They know how to fall without getting hurt," said Encyclopedia. "But the throws are an act. Bugs couldn't toss Spike and Rocky if they didn't let him."

After a whirlwind five minutes, the Tigers lined up and bowed. Coach Richards stepped forward to thank them.

Bugs held up his hand. "I'm not finished," he said.

Coach Richards moved back, surprised.

Bugs repeated the grip on Rocky.

Spike strode toward Bugs. He stopped within a foot of his leader.

Bugs shot a hand to Spike's throat. When he pulled the hand away, Spike fell over on his back and did not move.

Bugs repeated the grip on Rocky. He, too, fell over on his back and lay unmoving.

"You just saw my super-secret hold," announced Bugs. "I completely knocked out Rocky and Spike. But I didn't hurt them. If I really wanted to, though, I could break their necks for life."

Rocky and Spike stirred. They crawled off the mat shaking their heads.

The gym had grown silent. All eyes were on Bugs.

"Now you're asking yourselves, 'Where did Bugs learn this terrible hold?'" he continued. "I'll tell you. I wrote to a famous professor in Japan for the secret."

Bugs strutted up and down the mat. "A lot of you have heard about a certain girl who is supposed to have licked me," he went on. "Now you know I wasn't trying. I could have put her in the hospital, only I'm a gentleman."

His meaning was clear, and all the children understood. Bugs was challenging Sally to a rematch, then and there! If Sally refused to fight, or if she were beaten, Bugs would rule the neighborhood. The Brown Detective Agency would be powerless to halt his bullying.

A small boy near Sally pleaded, "Don't fight him. He could *kill* you!"

But Encyclopedia whispered into Sally's ear. As she listened, her lips tightened. "Super-secret hold, phooey!" she snorted. A moment later she was on the mat.

Bugs turned white. He had thought to scare her. Now *he* was the one who was scared.

There was nothing for him to do but fight. He reached for Sally's throat and took a thump in the stomach.

Fortunately for Bugs, his two-week course in judo had taught him how to fall. Sally's fists gave him plenty of practice. Eventually he lay on his back and refused to get up.

"I can't go on," he wailed. "I hurt my back lifting a big box this morning."

"He must have hurt his head," thought Encyclopedia, "to believe anyone would fall for his super-secret hold!"

WHY DIDN'T ENCYCLOPEDIA BELIEVE THE HOLD?

(*Turn to page 88 for the solution to the Case of the Super-Secret Hold.*)

The Case of the Wagon Master

"Sssh!" whispered Sally. "I think we are about to be attacked."

Encyclopedia listened. He heard a faint rustle of leaves outside the Brown Detective Agency. But he could see no one.

"It must be Joe Cooper," he said quietly.

For a long time nothing happened. Then a voice barked, "Bang! Bang!"

From behind the bush jumped a boy dressed like Daniel Boone. He wore a suit of buckskin, a coonskin cap, and moccasins with colored beads. He was aiming a rusty old rifle at the detectives.

"Joe Cooper!" scolded Sally. "You shouldn't go around scaring people like that!"

"I'm on the warpath," announced Joe.

Joe came from one of Idaville's oldest families. The Coopers had settled in the area when it was still overrun by palmetto palms and Indians. Whenever Joe felt mad at anybody, he went "on the warpath." He dressed up like a frontiersman and pretended to shoot his enemy. It made him feel better.

"I could have filled you both with holes," he said proudly.

Encyclopedia knew Joe's rifle was so old and rusted it couldn't shoot gumdrops. "I'm glad you missed," he said, playing along.

"I missed you on purpose," said Joe. "It's not you I'm mad at today. It's Buck Calhoun."

"Holy cats!" exclaimed Encyclopedia. "Buck Calhoun has been dead for a hundred years. You can't shoot *him!*"

"Of course not! What do you think is making me so mad?" shouted Joe. Then, in a calmer voice he said, "Did you see the story about him in the newspaper this morning?"

Encyclopedia nodded. The newspaper re-

"I want to hire you," Joe said.

ported that a statue of Buck Calhoun had been unveiled at Fort Hope. The statue honored Buck's quick thinking in saving a wagon train in 1872.

"They've made a hero out of that bird-brained phoney!" said Joe. "Why, he was too stupid to stay with the Army as an Indian scout. He led the Fourth Cavalry into so many ambushes the troopers figured he was half redskin and half blind."

Joe slapped twenty-five cents on the gasoline can.

"I want to hire you," he said. "My great-grandfather was wounded because of Buck Calhoun, and he had to retire from the Army. Prove Buck *wasn't* a hero! Then they'll have to tear down the statue of him."

"We can only do our best," said Encyclopedia carefully.

After the terrible-tempered Joe had left, Sally questioned Encyclopedia.

"Do you think we should have taken his money?" she asked. "This isn't an ordinary case.

Where do we begin?"

"At Fort Hope," said Encyclopedia. "Let's go."

Fort Hope stood eleven miles west of Idaville. The fort had been entirely rebuilt so that it looked exactly as it had looked in 1872.

As Encyclopedia and Sally got off the bus, they saw that the three o'clock tour of the fort was underway. A man in a black cap was guiding a small group of people to the many points of interest.

"Just in time!" said Encyclopedia.

The guide had stopped at the statue of Buck Calhoun. The detectives joined the group and listened to the tale of that desperate midnight in July, 1872.

"Buck Calhoun was a scout for the Fourth Cavalry before he became a famous wagon train master," began the guide. "Early in July, the Seminoles put on the war paint. Calhoun knew they were burning and scalping, and when he came through that mountain pass, he took a long, hard look at Fort Hope."

The guide turned and pointed to the mountain pass, which was now Emerson Avenue.

"Despite a light rain, Calhoun had a good view of the fort from up in the pass," went on the guide. "The American flag was flying proudly, and soldiers manned the walls. Everything looked all right."

The guide paused to allow the group to get the feeling of danger. Then he resumed.

"Calhoun was wagon-train master for five hundred settlers. Having studied the fort from the distance, he decided it was safe to move from the pass. So shortly after midnight he started down. Only he didn't know the truth. The redskins had slain everyone inside the fort. What Calhoun saw were Indians dressed up in the uniforms of the dead soldiers!"

A woman in the group let out a shriek of horror. The guide gave her a comforting look and went on.

"When the settlers got onto the open ground, the Indians poured out of the fort, hollering and whooping and shooting. Half the settlers were

THE CASE OF THE WAGON MASTER

killed right off. The rest seemed doomed. But Calhoun stayed cool and did some fancy thinking. He closed up the big Conestoga wagons into columns of two's and raced for the fort's open gates."

A hush fell upon the group. No one moved. Everyone waited to hear the outcome of Buck Calhoun's heroic charge for the gates.

"Just as Calhoun figured," said the guide, "there wasn't enough room going through the gates for the skinniest Indian to sneak in alongside the big wagons. Suddenly all the settlers were inside the fort. And when Calhoun slammed the gates shut, all the Indians were outside. His courage, coolness, and quick thinking had saved half the settlers."

"You mean," spoke up Encyclopedia, "his stupidity *killed* half the settlers. He never should have led the wagon train down from the pass."

WHY NOT?

(*Turn to page 89 for the solution to the Case of the Wagon Master.*)

The Case of Sir Biscuit-Shooter

Lionel Fisk came into the Brown Detective Agency walking on his hands.

Encyclopedia knew what an upside-down Lionel meant. The circus was in town!

Lionel was the only boy in Idaville who wanted to be an acrobat. He could read an entire comic book while standing on his head.

"I brought you two tickets to the circus," he said, falling to his feet. "For you and Sally."

"Boy, thanks," said Encyclopedia. "They must have cost a lot."

Lionel shook his head. "My Uncle Barney sent them to me," he said proudly.

Encyclopedia knew about Lionel's Uncle

Barney. He had sold used cars, he had sold houses, and he had gone to prison for two years. Uncle Barney hadn't cheated people more than most men who sold used cars or houses. But he had been caught.

"Uncle Barney is working as a clown now," said Lionel. "After the show, I'll introduce you to him."

Lionel did five back flips and was out the door.

After lunch, Encyclopedia told Sally the good news. The partners caught the two o'clock bus to the circus grounds.

Lionel was there to greet them. He led them into the main tent and up the grandstand steps. The free seats were in the very last row. When the circus started, Encyclopedia scratched himself a few times. The center ring was so far away that even the elephants looked like trained fleas.

Lionel wriggled with delight when the clowns came on. His Uncle Barney first appeared as the rear end of a horse. Later, wearing pots and pans for armor, he clanked about as the fearless English knight, Sir Godfrey Biscuit-Shooter.

When the circus ended, Lionel took Encyclopedia and Sally behind the sideshow tents to meet Uncle Barney. Trailers, in which the performers lived and traveled, were parked in three rows.

"Hold it," said Encyclopedia suddenly. "There's some kind of trouble over there."

He pointed to a trailer with a lion's head painted on the side. A small group of circus people were gathered at the open door. Someone hollered, "Get the doctor!"

"And get that new clown Barney!" shouted Kitty, the bareback rider. She was dressed in a tight pink costume and soft slippers. "He's the one who did it!"

The three children moved toward the crowd. "Uncle Barney's in some kind of trouble," said Lionel in a worried tone.

As the doctor arrived, a woman in a house-